NICK®

SpongeBob SquarePants™

Phonics Reading Program
Book 12 : au, ai

D0097512

HAPPY BIRTHDAY, SQUIDWARD!

SCHOLASTIC

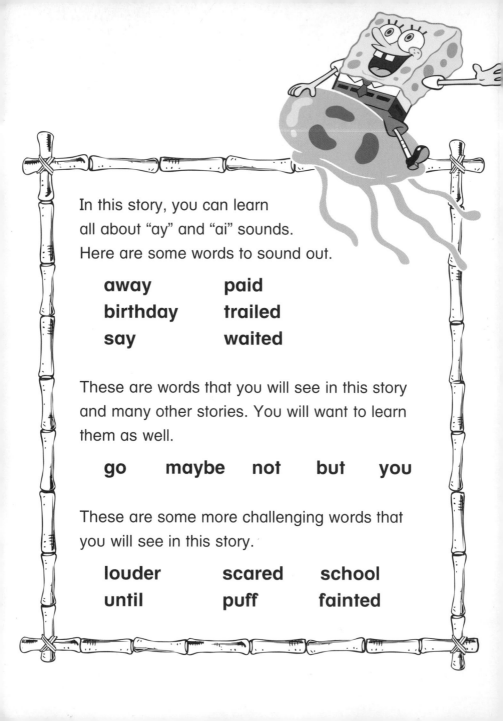

In this story, you can learn
all about "ay" and "ai" sounds.
Here are some words to sound out.

away	**paid**
birthday	**trailed**
say	**waited**

These are words that you will see in this story
and many other stories. You will want to learn
them as well.

go **maybe** **not** **but** **you**

These are some more challenging words that
you will see in this story.

louder	**scared**	**school**
until	**puff**	**fainted**

HAPPY BIRTHDAY, SQUIDWARD!

by Sonia Sander

SCHOLASTIC INC.

New York   Toronto   London   Auckland   Sydney
Mexico City   New Delhi   Hong Kong   Buenos Aires

"Patrick, look,"
said SpongeBob.
"Today is Squidward's
birthday! Let's go
wish him a happy day."

"Hooray! It's your birthday!"
said SpongeBob
and Patrick.
But Squidward ran away.
"Maybe he didn't hear us.
Maybe we need to
say it louder."

SpongeBob and Patrick
trailed Squidward
all the way to
Mrs. Puff's school.
They watched him go in
and then waited for him
to come back outside.

"Hip! Hip! Hooray!"
they yelled.
But it wasn't Squidward.
It was Mrs. Puff.
They scared her so much
that she fainted.
*Mmm. Maybe he's not
here,* they thought.

SpongeBob and Patrick followed Squidward's trail to the Krusty Krab. When they found Squidward inside, they sang "Happy Birthday" to him so loudly that they scared everyone away.

"None of them paid!"
yelled Mr. Krabs.
He blamed Squidward.
"You must find a way to pay
for all these meals."

"Please go away,"
  said Squidward.
"I do not like birthdays."
"We are going to stay
  outside today until
  you let us sing you
  'Happy Birthday,'" said
  SpongeBob.

"If you can't beat them,
join them," Squidward said.